DUE DATE

A PLACE FOR
GRACE

BY **Jean Davies Okimoto**

ILLUSTRATED BY
Doug Keith

SASQUATCH BOOKS
Seattle

To Katie and Sarah
— J.D.O.

To Beth and Corie Lyn
— D.K.

"Someday that will be me," dreamed Grace. "When I grow up, I'll be known as Grace: Amazing Guide Dog for the Blind."

"I will guide my owner with sure, strong steps. I will be brave, loyal, and true. I might even end up in the Animal Hall of Fame."

"But I must be prepared for guide dog school," Grace decided. "I will practice."

Grace sat and studied the traffic. She looked both ways and crossed when it was clear. She practiced at the corner of Geary and Powell, she practiced on the corner of Pine and Grant. She even practiced at Ghirardelli Square.

Finally September came, and Grace was ready for school.
"This is my big moment," she said to herself.

Grace found a place at the end of the row. She paid perfect attention as the trainer read the roll. "Abraham L., Eleanor R., Harriet T., Winston C., Colin P., Grace . . . Grace? GRACE!"

The trainer marched over
to Grace. "The students here
must be twenty inches tall.
You, little dog, are much too
small!"

Poor Grace.

She sat at the corner, wondering what to do.

Suddenly she heard the scream of a siren. Everyone
stopped. Everyone except the boy with the ball!

Grace leaped through the air and knocked the boy back to
the curb. . . . Safe!

Grace didn't know, but someone special had been
watching.

"I must get that dog," thought the man named Charlie.

But just as Charlie raced down the street, the Animal Control van appeared. Usually Grace was an expert at running away from the blue-and-white van . . . but not today.

Charlie was too late. Grace was caught!

Charlie rushed to the office of the Hearing Dog Program. "Mrs. Lombardi," Charlie signed, "today I saw a dog with the right stuff. She'd be a perfect student for your school. But she's landed in the pound."

"Are you quite sure she's hearing-dog material?" signed Mrs. Lombardi.

"From what I just saw, I'd bet on this dog," he replied.

"This is most unusual, Charlie, but I know you're tired of waiting for a hearing dog. I suppose we could give her a try."

Mrs. Lombardi and Charlie went to the Animal Control Shelter. They quickly found Grace and sprung her from the cage.

Charlie held Grace. Grace licked his face. "I must say, it seems to be love at first sight," signed Mrs. Lombardi. "But it will all depend on how she does in school."

The next day, Charlie fixed Grace a nice big breakfast. She liked the breakfast, but most of all she liked the man who talked with his hands.

"Good luck and study hard," Charlie signed. He hugged her good-bye and dropped her off in front of the school.

"Hearing dogs must be small and sprightly. When you hear certain sounds, you must jump lightly," said Mrs. Lombardi.

"This is the school for me," thought Grace. "I will be brave, loyal, and true to Charlie. Soon I'll be known as Grace: Amazing Hearing Dog!"

Wake Up was the first class. The dogs were taught to wake their owners. They jumped on them when the alarm clock rang.

Microwave was the next class. When the microwave beeped, they learned to lead to the kitchen.

Then came Phone Class. They learned to jump and lead at the sound of the TDD, a special phone for deaf people.

In Doorbell Class, they were taught to jump and lead to the door.

Smoke Alarm Class was the most important. When the smoke alarm screeched, they learned to leap and leap and leap.

"How's Grace doing?" Charlie asked after six weeks.

"Not very well," signed Mrs. Lombardi. "She has an A in Smoke Alarm and Phone, but when the microwave beeps she runs to the door, and when the doorbell rings she runs to the microwave."

"What about Wake Up?" Charlie asked.

"She flunks."

"What does she do?"

"She jumps on the bed and goes to sleep. We'll have to send Grace back to the pound," continued Mrs. Lombardi. "She will make someone a nice pet. But Grace simply doesn't have what it takes to make it here."

REPORT CARD
NAME: LOUIS

WAKE UP	A
DOORBELL	A
MICROWAVE	A
SMOKE ALARM	A
PHONE (TDD)	A

"We have a splendid new student who can be your hearing dog. Louis is at the top of his class—he leads to the door in three seconds flat! Truly outstanding!"

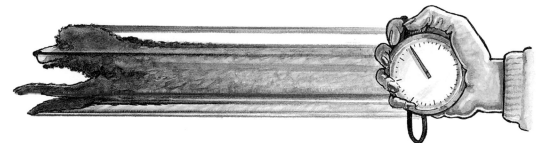

Charlie looked at Louis, then he looked at Grace.

Grace growled at Louis.

"She can't quit yet," signed Charlie. "I'm sure Grace just needs some extra help."

"Grace, this doorbell will never sound like a microwave beep," signed Charlie, after he bought a gong from his friend Eric Eng.

Grace listened carefully while Charlie bonged the gong. They practiced and practiced, then practiced some more.

When Grace got it right ninety-six gongs in a row, Charlie made a call on his special phone.

"Mrs. Lombardi," he typed, "please come and give Grace another chance."

GIVE GRACE ANOTHER CHANCE

MRS. LOMBARDI, PLEASE

"This is highly irregular," Mrs. Lombardi typed back, "but since you insist, I'll give her the test."

Grace passed Phone and Smoke Alarm. Then Mrs. Lombardi went to the kitchen and set the microwave.

Beep-beep, went the oven. Grace jumped on Charlie and led him straight to the kitchen.

Next, Mrs. Lombardi went to the door and hit Charlie's gong. There was no mistaking the bong for a beep! Grace jumped on Charlie, then led right to the door.

"The last test is Wake Up," signed Mrs. Lombardi. Charlie got in bed. Mrs. Lombardi set the alarm. *Riiinnnng!* went the clock. Grace jumped on the bed.

Grace went to sleep.

"It's too bad Grace didn't pass," signed Mrs. Lombardi on her way out the door. "But you can still have our top dog, Louis . . . the best and the brightest."

"I'll never give up on Grace," signed Charlie.

The next day, Charlie called Mrs. Lombardi on the special phone. "I bought a new clock. I'm sure now that Grace can pass!"

"I hope this isn't a waste of time," signed Mrs. Lombardi, as Charlie set the clock and got in bed.

Riiiing! went the clock. Grace jumped on Charlie and licked his face. Charlie tapped the top of the clock. Grace snuggled next to Charlie and began to snooze. Charlie snoozed, too.

Riiiing! went the clock. Grace sat up and licked Charlie's face. Charlie tapped the top of the clock. They snuggled and snoozed some more.

Riiiing! Grace sat up and licked Charlie's face. Charlie tapped the top of the clock. "We can't lie here all day, Grace," he signed, and they jumped out of bed.

"This is most unusual," signed Mrs. Lombardi, "but Grace here seems to be a snooze alarm. I guess we can say she's passed the class."

Graduation day came. Grace sat on the stage with the rest of the students. They wore bright orange coats that proclaimed they were hearing dogs. Everyone cheered and cheered.

After the ceremony the owners came up and got their dogs. Charlie held Grace. Grace licked his face.

"It's time to come home and take your place," Charlie signed, "my official hearing dog . . . snooze-alarm Grace."

Printed in Hong Kong

Designed by Judythe Sieck

Library of Congress Cataloging in Publication Data
Okimoto, Jean Davies.
    A place for Grace / by Jean Davies Okimoto : illustrated by Doug
Keith.
        p.   cm.
        Summary: With the help of a hearing-impaired man, a little dog
finally manages to graduate from a training school for hearing dogs.
        ISBN 0-912365-73-0 : $14.95
        [1. Hearing ear dogs—Fiction.   2. Dogs—Fiction.   3. Deaf—
Fiction.   4. Physically handicapped—Fiction.]   I. Keith, Doug,
PZ7.0415P1   1993
[E]—dc20   92-42588
                                                                    CIP
                                                                     AC

Sasquatch Books
1931 Second Avenue
Seattle, Washington 98101
(206) 441-5555

*Special thanks to Marianne Dondero
at the San Francisco SPCA Hearing Dog Program.*